Copyright © 1983 by Parker Brothers, Division of CPG Products Corp. All rights reserved.
Published in the United States by Parker Brothers, Division of CPG Products Corp.

Strawberry Shortcake Characters and Designs © 1983 American Greetings Corporation. TM* designates trademarks of American Greetings Corporation.

Library of Congress Cataloging in Publication Data: Miller, Nell. Strawberry Shortcake and the crazy baking contest. SUMMARY: Hoping to disrupt the baking contest, the Purple Pieman slips some silly juice into one of the pies that is being judged.
[1. Contests—Fiction] I. Sustendal, Pat, ill.
II. Title. PZ7.M6315St 1983 [E] 83-8101 ISBN 0-910313-09-1
Manufactured in the United States of America   1 2 3 4 5 6 7 8 9 0

Strawberry Shortcake

and the Crazy Baking Contest

Story by Nell Miller
Pictures by Pat Sustendal

One morning as Strawberry Shortcake and her little
kitten, Custard, were taking a walk, they saw a large sign.

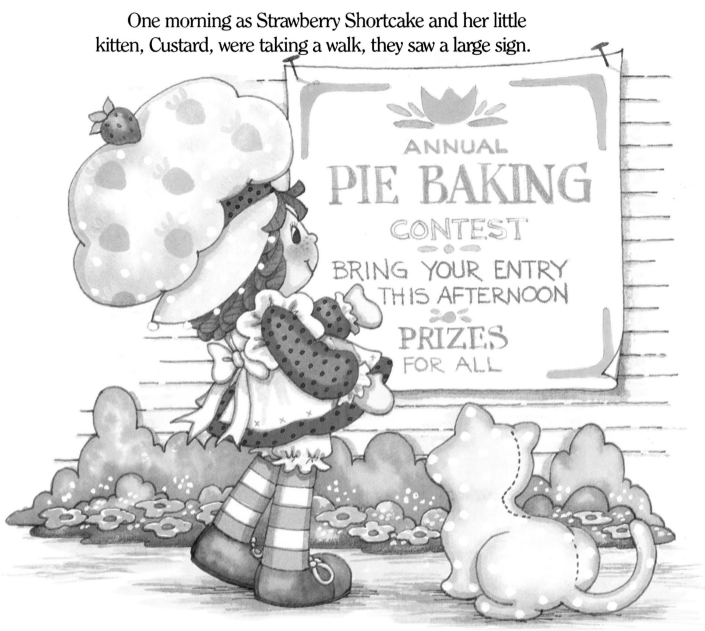

"Look, Custard," Strawberry said pointing to the sign.
Of course, Custard couldn't read. But she sat in front of
the sign purring.

"I must make a large strawberry pie to enter in the
contest," said Strawberry Shortcake.

As they walked back towards home, they met several of their friends. Everyone was excited about the pie baking contest.

"Guess what kind of pie I'm going to make?" asked Huckleberry Pie.

Everyone laughed. That was such an easy question to answer. "I'm going to bake a pie too," said Raspberry Tart. Her little monkey, Rhubarb, rubbed his stomach with delight.

"I shall bake a pie too," said Almond Tea, who was standing nearby.

Almond Tea was such a fine baker that Strawberry Shortcake didn't think anyone else would have much chance to win the contest. However, it would still be fun to enter. Besides, the sign had said, "Prizes for All!"

When they returned home, Strawberry took a basket from her cupboard and went out into her garden to pick some berries. There were so many big, ripe berries growing that she would have enough for as many pies as she wanted.

As she picked, Strawberry Shortcake thought about the contest. She wondered how she could make a fruit pie that would be different. While she carefully walked up and down the rows selecting only the largest and juiciest strawberries, Custard ran about through the plants.

Strawberry Shortcake looked up to see Lucky Bug flying overhead. "Good morning, Lucky Bug," she called to her tiny friend. "You slept very late this morning. I'm picking berries to make a pie for the pie contest."

Custard was feeling very playful and tried to catch the little
lady bug. Strawberry stopped her picking to watch them.
Custard looked so funny jumping into the air trying to catch
Lucky Bug. But no matter how high Custard jumped, Lucky
Bug could fly higher.

Then Custard lost her balance and fell right into the
basket that Strawberry had filled with berries.

"Oh, you silly kitten," laughed Strawberry Shortcake.
"Now I will have custard with my strawberries."

As she said the words, Strawberry Shortcake realized that
she had discovered what kind of pie to make. Of course! A
strawberry custard pie would be even more delicious than a
plain strawberry pie. She was delighted with this new plan and
bent down to pick more berries.

Strawberry Shortcake was so busy picking her berries that she didn't see the Purple Pieman as he sneaked past her garden. He was angry, for all of the Kids in Strawberryland were busy working in their gardens, picking berries for their contest pies. It was impossible for him to steal any berries today, so he could not make a pie for the contest. "I will think of a way to spoil this pie baking contest," he said to himself. "Why should the Kids have all the fun of winning prizes?"

As soon as Strawberry Shortcake finished picking her berries she went inside and set to work on her pie. First she made a fine crust, using flour and butter, and lined it with strawberries. Then she prepared a delicious custard. She mixed fresh eggs and rich milk and sugar in a large bowl. Custard jumped up on the counter to watch. She hoped that Strawberry Shortcake would save a little milk for her to lick up.

When the custard was ready, Strawberry poured it over the strawberries in the pie crust and set the pie in the oven to bake. When it was done, she added more strawberries all around the top. They looked like bright red jewels against the creamy yellow color of the custard.

"Oh Custard," said Strawberry, "as soon as the pie cools I will take it to the contest." Custard purred loudly. She was proud to have helped Strawberry think of the idea of a strawberry custard pie.

Strawberry Shortcake put her pie on the window ledge to cool. Then she went to change her clothes. She had spilled a little custard on her dress when she was working and she wanted to look as fresh and as lovely as her pie.

Custard stayed in the kitchen licking out the bowl. As she licked the rim, she heard a sound. It was the Purple Pieman standing by the window. The Pieman was sniffing the strawberry custard pie. "This pie looks too good," he said. "I had better fix it a little."

Then the Purple Pieman put his hand into his pocket and pulled out a bottle of silly juice. He looked to see if anyone was watching. No one was there except Custard. "Well, Cat," he said. "You can't tell on me." Quickly he opened the bottle and poured some of the silly juice onto the pie. The silly juice went right into the custard, and you couldn't see or smell it at all.

"No one will ever guess what I did,"
said the Purple Pieman, "and whoever
eats it will become *so* silly." He laughed
and rushed off.

Custard ran into the next room to tell Strawberry what had happened. But though she meowed and meowed, Strawberry Shortcake did not understand at all.

"You sound just as excited about this contest as I feel," she said to her little kitten.

Then very carefully, Strawberry Shortcake lifted her pie from the window ledge and walked with it towards the contest. When she arrived, she could see that there were many wonderful entries to compete with hers.

To Strawberry's surprise, the contest judge was Almond Tea. "I couldn't enter the contest after all," said Almond Tea, "because I was asked to be the judge."

"That's because you are such a wonderful baker," said Strawberry.

Strawberry's heart beat with excitement. Perhaps she
would have a chance to win now that Almond Tea wasn't in
the contest.

Almond Tea cut a thin piece from each pie. "One way to judge a pie is to see how it slices and how the crust holds together," she explained. Everyone was surprised. The only way they knew to judge a pie was by eating it.

"Of course I'll taste the pies too," said Almond Tea, "but first I want to examine their appearance."

As Almond Tea took the slices to the side to look at them, the Purple Pieman approached. The Pieman smiled when he noticed that a slice was missing from the strawberry custard pie. He looked around to see what silly things were being done.

He saw nothing.

That was most strange. It was impossible to eat a slice of pie with silly juice on it without becoming very silly. He began to wonder if he had poured the wrong thing on Strawberry's pie. He thought that he had better find out.

The Purple Pieman reached out and cut himself a large piece of the strawberry custard pie.

"Are you a judge in this contest too?" asked Blueberry Muffin.

"I am the best pie judge in the world," the Purple Pieman said as he swallowed a large mouthful of pie. "I can judge pies every which way!" he shouted as he suddenly stood on his head and grabbed for another slice.

"Stop!" Almond Tea called to him. "I need to have a taste of it too." She reached for the pie just as the Pieman began to jump up and down and oink like a pig. He knocked her hand, and the rest of the strawberry custard pie fell on the ground.

"Oh, whatever is wrong with that silly Pieman?" cried Strawberry sadly. "Now no one will be able to eat my pie."

She was wrong. Even though none of the Kids ate it, Custard, Pupcake the dog, Cheesecake the mouse and Rhubarb the monkey quickly rushed up and began to gobble the pie.

"Eat up! Eat up!" shouted the Purple Pieman who was waddling like a duck with a bucket on his head. And they did.

Then even more strange and silly things began to happen. Custard began to balance on one paw. Cheesecake began to twirl her tail like a lasso.

Rhubarb started to dance like a ballerina, and Pupcake
tried to climb a tree while he chattered like a monkey.

"Oh, help!" cried the Pieman. "The silly juice that I put in the pie is making everything too silly."

He and the pets looked so funny that while
Strawberry Shortcake knew she should be
angry with him, she couldn't help but
laugh and laugh. Now she didn't even
mind that she couldn't win the contest.

After a little while the silly juice wore off and everything calmed down again. Then Almond Tea said, "The best looking pie was the strawberry custard baked by Strawberry Shortcake. Even though I didn't taste it, I am awarding her a special blue ribbon. Now everyone else can eat some of all these other wonderful pies, so everyone will be a winner."

Everyone was very pleased. Then Strawberry Shortcake
said something that made them even happier. She said,
"Tomorrow I am going to make several of my special
strawberry custard pies, and everyone here is invited
to come to a tea party and see that they
taste as good as they look."

"Am I invited too?" begged the Purple Pieman, who was again standing on his head.

"Do you promise to wait your turn and sit properly at the table and play no tricks at all?" asked Strawberry.

"I promise. I promise," said the Purple Pieman. "I will be very good."

"Then you may come too," said Strawberry Shortcake.

But do you think the Purple Pieman really kept his promise?